Frozen Noses

by JAN CARR

illustrated by

DOROTHY DONOHUE

Holiday House / New York

Book design by Sylvia Frezzolini Severance

Library of Congress Cataloging-in-Publication Data

Carr, Jan.
        Frozen noses / by Jan Carr;
illustrated by Dorothy Donohue.
              p.   cm.
    Summary: Describes the delights of such winter activities as
throwing snowballs, making a snowman, and going ice skating.
        ISBN 0-8234-1462-0
        [1. Winter—Fiction.   2. Stories in rhyme.]
I. Donohue, Dorothy, ill.   II. Title.
PZ8.3.C19955Fr   1999
{E}—dc21   98-48540
                           CIP
                           AC

3487 9766 3/07

For Charlie, who was born in a light flurry of snow,
and for Mom, who shines in winter
— J. C.

To my buddy Janet,
to Regina for her trust,
and in memory of my sweet Megga May
— D. D.

Frozen noses
Tingly toeses

Sniffle, snuffle
Winter's cold!

Better bundle!
Quiver, shiver
Booted, buckled
Buttonholed

Snowballs, throw balls
Pack and stack them
Roly-poly
Chubby chap

Coal for eyes
A proper topper
Whoosh of wind
Whoa! Catch that hat!

Onward! Upward!
I'm a climber!
Scramble up
Heave-ho the rope!

Veer down, steer down
Whee, I'm whizzing!
Thump a-bump
The slippery slope

Lace my skates up
Tie them tightly
Ready, steady
I won't fall

Slide, collide
Get good at gliding
Hit a skid
Whoops! All a-sprawl!

Sun sets early
Sky's a-swirly
Clouds collect–
Another storm?

Bundle blankets
Crackle, kindle
Cup of cocoa—

Winter warm.